CLASSICS Illustrated®

STEPHEN CRANE
THE RED BADGE OF COURAGE

essay by
Julie Bleha
Columbia University

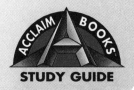

ACCLAIM BOOKS
STUDY GUIDE

The Red Badge of Courage
Originally published as Classics Illustrated no. 98
Art by Gustav Schrotter

"An Outline History of the Civil War" Art by Maurice del Bourgo

Adaption by Ken Fitch
Cover by John Paul Leon

For Classics Illustrated Study Guides
computer recoloring by Colorpillar
editor: Madeleine Robins
assistant editor: Gregg Sanderson
design: Scott Friedlander

Dale-Chall R.L.: 6.5

ISBN 1-57840-040-6

Acclaim Books, New York, NY
Printed in the United States

The RED BADGE of COURAGE

by **STEPHEN CRANE**

THIS IS NO EPIC HISTORY OF GENERALS, GLORIOUS VICTORIES, OR DIRE DEFEATS. THIS IS SIMPLY THE STORY OF WHAT BEFELL ONLY ONE YOUNG LAD ON THAT FATEFUL DAY WHEN HE CAME FACE-TO-FACE WITH THE MONSTER CALLED WAR.

IN THE SPRING OF 1861, JUST AFTER THE START OF THE CIVIL WAR, HENRY FLEMING WENT PEACEFULLY ABOUT HIS CHORES ON HIS MOTHER'S FARM. IN HIS THOUGHTS, THOUGH, HE SAW HIMSELF ON THE BATTLEFIELD, PERFORMING SHINING DEEDS OF BRAVERY.

FINALLY, ONE NIGHT...

MA, I'M GOING TO ENLIST.

HENRY, DON'T YOU BE A FOOL. NOW, GO BACK TO SLEEP.

NEVERTHELESS, THE FOLLOWING MORNING...

U.S. ARMY RECRUITING STATION ENLIST HERE!

WHEN HENRY RETURNED HOME...

MA, I'VE ENLISTED.

THE LORD'S WILL BE DONE.

YOU WATCH OUT, HENRY, AN' TAKE GOOD KEER OF YORSELF IN THIS HERE FIGHTIN' BUSINESS. DON'T GO A-THINKIN' YOU CAN LICK THE HULL REBEL ARMY. AN' ALLUS BE KEERFUL AN' CHOOSE YER COMP'NY. DON'T EVER DO ANYTHING YOU WOULD BE 'SHAMED TO LET ME KNOW ABOUT. ALSO, NEVER DO NO SHIRKING ON MY ACCOUNT. IF SO BE A TIME COMES WHEN YOU HAVE TO BE KILT, DON'T THINK OF ANYTHING 'CEPT WHAT'S RIGHT, BECAUSE THERE'S MANY A WOMAN HAS TO BEAR UP 'GINST SECH THINGS THESE TIMES, AN' THE LORD'LL TAKE KEER OF US ALL.

LATER THAT NIGHT...

I TELL YOU. THERE'LL BE A REAL BATTLE TOMORROW. THE CAVALRY LEFT THIS MORNING -- GOING TO RICHMOND WHILE WE FIGHT THE REBS HERE.

THUNDER! I HOPE YOU'RE RIGHT, JIM.

GO ON, CONKLIN, YA SAID THE SAME THING LAST WEEK.

SUDDENLY UNEASY AT THE NEWS, HENRY BEGAN TO WONDER IF HIS COURAGE WOULD FAIL HIM DURING THE IMPENDING BATTLE...

JIM, THINK ANY OF THE BOYS WILL RUN?

WELL, A FEW MAYBE. OF COURSE, THE HULL KIT-AND-BOODLE MIGHT RUN, FIRST TIME THEY GIT SHOT AT. BUT I FIGGER THEY'LL BE ALL RIGHT ONCE THEY GIT T' SHOOTIN'.

DO YOU-- DO YOU THINK YOU MIGHT RUN, JIM?

WELL, IF A LOT OF OTHERS RUN, PROB'LY I'D RUN. BUT IF EVER'BODY WAS A-STANDIN' AND A-FIGHTIN', I'D FIGHT TOO.

HUH! BET YA'D RUN LIKE A JACKRABBIT. NOT ME! I JUST WISH THEY'D LET ME AT 'EM. THAT'S ALL!

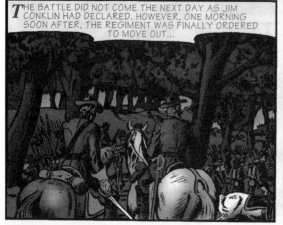

THE BATTLE DID NOT COME THE NEXT DAY AS JIM CONKLIN HAD DECLARED. HOWEVER, ONE MORNING SOON AFTER, THE REGIMENT WAS FINALLY ORDERED TO MOVE OUT...

WE'RE IN FOR IT NOW. THEY'RE TAKING US OUT TO GET SLAUGHTERED. WHY DIDN'T I LISTEN TO MA AND STAY HOME?

SAY, WILSON, DO YOU THINK YOU'D SKEDADDLE IF THE JOHNNIES WAS TO CHARGE YOU?

NOT A CHANCE, HENRY. THE MAN THAT BETS ON MY RUNNIN' WILL LOSE HIS MONEY.

YOU'LL GET YOUR CHANCE SOON, WILSON. WE'RE ACROSS THE RIVER AND WILL PROBABLY COME UP ON THEM FROM BEHIND.

CAN'T COME SOON ENOUGH FOR ME.

*B*UT THE REGIMENT MARCHED FOR MANY DAYS. WHILE THE OTHER MEN GRUMBLED ABOUT SORE FEET AND SHORT RATIONS, HENRY CONTINUED TO WORRY ABOUT RUNNING FROM BATTLE. FINALLY, ONE GRAY DAWN, HENRY WAS AWAKENED BY A KICK...

COME ON, HENRY. WE'RE MOVIN' AGAIN. HURRY!

WHAT'S UP, JIM? WHERE WE RUSHIN' IN SUCH AN ALL-FIRED HURRY?

IT'S THE REAL THING THIS TIME. THE HULL BRIGADE IS FORMING OVER THE HILL.

NO WAY OUT NOW. I'M TRAPPED... IT'S LIKE BEING IN A MOVING BOX.

THIS IS NO PLACE FOR A BATTLEFIELD. IT'S - IT'S TOO SMALL. WHAT KIND OF OFFICERS HAVE WE GOT ANYHOW?

ALL RIGHT, MEN. WE'RE HEADING FOR THE OTHER SIDE OF THE WOODS. SPREAD OUT WIDE!

IT'S STUPID TO ADVANCE OVER AN OPEN FIELD. I OUGHT TO WARN THEM. THEY DON'T REALIZE...

GET ALONG THERE, YOU! NO SKULKING HERE!

AFTER A TIME, THE BRIGADE WAS HALTED...

DIG IN, MEN! WE'LL HOLD THESE POSITIONS!

BUT SOON AS THEY WERE DUG IN, THE ORDER CAME TO MOVE OUT AGAIN...

FIRST THEY SAY "DIG IN" AND THEN "MOVE ON". WHY DON'T THEY MAKE UP THEIR MINDS?

AGAIN CAME THE ORDER TO "DIG IN"...

FINE KIND O' WAR! WHEN WE GOIN' TO DO SOME FIGHTIN'? IF ANYONE WITH ANY SENSE WAS A-RUNNIN' THIS ARMY...

SHUT YER BIG TALK! YOU HAVEN'T HAD THAT THERE UNIFORM ON SIX MONTHS, WILSON, AND YOU TALK LIKE A GENERAL!

JUST THEN, THE ENEMY'S ARTILLERY OPENED FIRE...

GET DOWN, WILSON! YOU WANT TO GET KILLED, YOU DARN FOOL?

I'M-- I'M A GONER FOR SURE. I'LL NEVER GO HOME ALIVE. I KNOW IT.

AS THE BATTLE RAGED, A SOLDIER NEAR HENRY TURNED AND STARTED TO RUN TOWARD THE REAR...

I DON'T WANT TO BE KILLED! I DON'T WANT TO DIE!

GET BACK THERE AND FIGHT OR I'LL CUT YOU DOWN!

AFTER WHAT SEEMED AN ETERNITY, THE FIRING SLOWED DOWN AND THE SMOKE CLEARED...

LOOK, WILSON, THEY'RE FALLING BACK! BY GUM, WE'VE HELD THEM!

THANK GOD, THANK GOD, IT'S OVER.

WE DONE IT, HENRY, WE DONE IT!

GUESS WE SHOWED THEM REBS, HUH, JIM? I'M GLAD IT'S OVER, THOUGH. SURE FEELS GOOD TO REST, DOESN'T IT?

BUT JUST A FEW SECONDS LATER...

HENRY! LOOK! THEY'RE COMING AGAIN!

WHAT? SO SOON? OH NO-NO!

IT ISN'T FAIR TO COME AT US AGAIN SO SOON. WE'LL NEVER STAND A SECOND BANGING.

TERRIFIED BY THE SECOND REBEL ONSLAUGHT, SEVERAL SOLDIERS NEAR HENRY TURNED FROM THE FIRING LINE AND TOOK TO THEIR HEELS...

THEY'RE ALL RUNNING... THEY'RE LEAVING ME ALONE. I WON'T STAY HERE AND GET BUTCHERED.

*H*ENRY DROPPED HIS RIFLE AND PACK AND RAN FROM THE SPOT AS FAST AS HIS FEAR-INSPIRED LEGS COULD TAKE HIM...

I'LL BE KILLED. I'VE GOT TO GET AWAY.

HALT! YOU THERE! STAND AND FIGHT!

*C*HOKING WITH FEAR AND DUST, HENRY FLED THROUGH THE WOODS AND STUMBLED BLINDLY INTO A TREE. PANIC-STRICKEN, BELIEVING THE ENEMY WAS AT HIS HEELS, HE GOT UP AND RAN AGAIN.

I CAN'T BE BLAMED FOR RUNNING -- THEY'RE ALL DOING IT. AT LEAST THOSE BEHIND ME WILL GET SHOT FIRST.

*F*ROM A SMALL RISE IN THE GROUND, HENRY SAW A BRIGADE GOING TO THE RELIEF OF HIS EMBATTLED COMPANIONS...

THE IDIOTS. WHY DON'T THEY RETREAT? THEY'LL ALL BE KILLED.

A WHILE LATER, HENRY CAME UPON TWO OFFICERS. HE CREPT CLOSE AND WAS AMAZED AT WHAT HE HEARD...

THEY'VE HELD 'EM, COLONEL! BY HEAVENS, THEY'VE HELD 'EM!

WHAT'S HE SAYING? WE WON? BUT-- IT CAN'T BE.

OVERWHELMED WITH SHAME AT HIS OWN COWARDICE, HENRY PLUNGED DEEPER INTO THE FOREST...

WE WON... AND I RAN. I'M A COWARD. I CAN'T GO BACK NOW. THEY'D LAUGH AT ME... AND IT ISN'T FAIR. I ONLY RAN BECAUSE I HAVE MORE SENSE THAN THE OTHERS. IT'S A NATURAL INSTINCT.

SPYING A SQUIRREL IN A TREE, HENRY HURLED A PINE CONE AT HIM. AS THE ANIMAL FLED IN TERROR, HENRY'S FAITH IN HIMSELF WAS PARTIALLY RESTORED...

THERE. THAT PROVES IT. EVEN A SQUIRREL'S GOT SENSE ENOUGH TO RUN FROM DANGER.

AS HE STUMBLED ALONG, HENRY SUDDENLY CAME FACE-TO-FACE WITH A DEAD INFANTRYMAN WHOSE APPEARANCE INDICATED THAT HE HAD BEEN DEAD QUITE SOME TIME...

E-E-E-YOW

JIMMINY. IT'S A CORPSE. HE- HE'S LOOKING AT ME.

TERRIFIED BY THE GRISLY SIGHT, HENRY BACKED SLOWLY AWAY FROM THE SPOT BEFORE AGAIN TAKING TO HIS HEELS IN PANIC...

IF I TURN MY BACK TOO SOON, HE MAY SPRING UP AND CHASE AFTER ME.

*H*ALF-MAD WITH PAIN FROM HIS WOUND AND TERRIFIED BY THE APPROACHING WAGONS, JIM SUDDENLY STAGGERED AWAY FROM HENRY AND FLED INTO THE OPEN FIELD...

JIMI JIM, WHERE YA GOIN'? STOP! YOU'LL HURT YERSELF!

HE'S RUNNIN' OFF. WHERE'S HE GET HIS STRENGTH? I DON'T SEE HOW HE CAN EVEN STAND WITH A HOLE IN HIS CHEST.

14-7TH ARTILLERY REGIMENT

*A*FTER A MOMENT OR TWO, JIM STOPPED AND TURNED TO FACE HIS PURSUERS...

JIMI WHAT'S THE MATTER? LET ME HELP YOU!

LEAVE ME BEI DON'T TOUCH ME! LEAVE ME BE!

OHHHH....

JIMI JIM!

WELL, HE WAS A REG'LAR JIM-DANDY FOR NERVE, WA'N'T HE? NEVER SEEN A MAN DO LIKE THAT BEFORE.

COME ON, SON. NO USE STAYIN' HERE. WE GOTTA GIT ALONG AN' GIT OUR WOUNDS TAKEN CARE OF!

HE WAS THE FIRST FRIEND THAT I HAD IN THE ARMY, I'D LIKE TO GET 'EM FOR THIS!

YE'RE LOOKIN' PRETTY PEEKED YERSELF, SON. COME ON. MEBBE YER HURT WORSE THAN YEH THINK. WHERE'S YER WOUND, EH?

HARASSED AND SHAMED BY THE MAN'S PERSISTENT QUESTIONING, HARRY BRUSHED HIM AWAY AND RAN OFF DOWN THE ROAD.

WHAT'S WRONG, BOY? WHERE YEH GOIN'?

DON'T BOTHER ME! JUST LEAVE ME ALONE!

AS HENRY ROUNDED A HILL, HE PERCEIVED THAT THE ROADWAY WAS NOW A DISPIRITED MASS OF WAGONS, TEAMS AND MEN... HE FELT SOMEWHAT COMFORTED BY THE SIGHT...

THEY ARE RETREATING. GUESS I WASN'T SO WRONG TO RUN AFTER ALL.

SOON, A SECOND COLUMN APPEARED ON THE ROAD... A FORWARD-GOING COLUMN. AS HENRY LOOKED AT THE FRESH, CONFIDENT TROOPS, THE BLACK WEIGHT OF HIS WOE RETURNED TO HIM...

THEY'RE ADVANCING. THEY'RE MOVING UP FRESH TROOPS. JIMINY, I'D LIKE TO BE WITH THEM. IF ONLY I WASN'T SUCH A COWARD.

WHY CAN'T I BE BRAVE LIKE THOSE FELLOWS? BUT EVEN IF I GO BACK TO THE REGIMENT, THE FELLOWS'LL CALL ME YELLOW AND LAUGH AT ME.

DURING THE LULL IN THE FIGHTING, HENRY AND WILSON WENT TO REPLENISH THEIR WATER SUPPLY. ON THE WAY, THEY CAME UPON TWO OF THEIR LEADERS DISCUSSING PLANS FOR FOR THE DIVISION'S NEXT MOVE...

COME ON, WILSON. I THOUGHT I SAW A STREAM DOWN THERE.

HOLD UP A BIT, HENRY. WE MIGHT CATCH WHAT THEM TWO ARE SAYIN'.

COLONEL, THE ENEMY IS FORMING FOR ANOTHER CHARGE. IT'LL BE DIRECTED AGAINST WHITERSIDE AND I FEAR THEY'LL BREAK THROUGH THERE UNLESS WE WORK LIKE THUNDER TO STOP THEM. WHAT TROOPS CAN YOU SPARE?

THERE'S THE 304th. THEY FIGHT LIKE A LOT 'A MULE DRIVERS. I CAN SPARE THEM BEST OF ANY.

VERY WELL, COLONEL, GET YOUR MULE DRIVERS READY. BUT I'M AFRAID NOT MANY OF THEM WILL COME BACK.

THRILLED BY THE FACT THAT FOR THE FIRST TIME THEY HAD ADVANCE INFORMATION, HENRY AND WILSON RUSHED BACK TO INFORM THEIR COMRADES...

WE'RE GOING TO CHARGE! WE JUST HEARD GENERAL THOMPSON TELL THE COLONEL!

SURE 'NOUGH, FLEMING?

AH, HE'S LYIN'. HE DOESN'T KNOW.

HOPE TO DIE. SURE AS SHOOTIN' I TELL YOU.

WE HEARD 'EM TALKING.

FIVE MINUTES LATER, THE BOYS' REPORT WAS CONFIRMED. THE REGIMENT WAS ASSEMBLED...

COME ON, WILSON! NOW WE'LL FIND OUT WHAT WAR IS REALLY LIKE!

BUT A DARK SHADOW CROSSED HENRY'S MIND AS THE DIN OF BATTLE BECAME ALMOST DEAFENING...

I WONDER IF THIS IS THE END. THE GENERAL SAID NOT MANY OF US WOULD COME BACK.

CHARGE!

THE MEN RACED ACROSS THE OPEN FIELD AS THE CONFEDERATE BATTERIES OPENED FIRE. STUNNED FOR A MOMENT BY THE IMMINENCE OF DEADLY PERIL, HENRY LAGGED BEHIND...

C'MON, YA LUNKHED! GET ACROSS THAT FIELD! DO YOU WANT TO STAND HERE AND GET SLAUGHTERED LIKE A MOONSTRUCK CALF?

*E*NRAGED AND INDIGNANT, HENRY SPRANG TO LIFE AND LED THE CHARGE ACROSS THE FIELD...

COME ON YOURSELF IF YOU'RE SO BRAVE!

THE FLAG! IT'S FALLING!

GOT IT, WILSON! LET'S GO!

*T*HE CONFEDERATE COMMANDERS RUSHED UP REINFORCEMENTS AND THE UNION CHARGE FALTERED. HENRY'S REGIMENT BEGAN TO FALL BACK AS THEIR OFFICERS RAGED AT THE MEN.

DIG IN, MEN! HERE THEY COME! WE CAN HOLD THEM IF YOU TRADE THEM SHOT FOR SHOT!

*T*HE TWO FORCES CRASHED TOGETHER FIERCELY IN THE CENTER OF THE FIELD. THE FIGHTING WAS BLOODY AND FURIOUS BUT THE REBELS WERE FINALLY PUSHED BACK.

*F*OLLOWING THIS HAND-TO-HAND ENCOUNTER, THERE WAS A BRIEF LULL IN THE FIGHTING...

WELL, WE DID IT. WE PUSHED THEM BACK.

I NEVER THOUGHT WE'D MAKE IT, HENRY. NO, BY JIMINY, I NEVER THOUGHT WE'D MAKE IT.

I DIDN'T TURN TAIL AND RUN THAT TIME, BY GINGER. MULE DRIVERS, ARE WE? HUH.

*B*UT THIS FEELING OF SELF-SATISFACTION WAS SHORT-LIVED...

THUNDER, WHAT AN AWFUL MESS YOU MADE, COLONEL MacCHESNAY! YOU STOPPED ABOUT A HUNDRED FEET SHORT OF OUR OBJECTIVE!

BUT, GENERAL--I'M SORRY, SIR. WE WENT AS FAR AS WE COULD.

AS FAR AS YOU COULD, EH? WELL, THAT WASN'T VERY FAR, WAS IT? WHAT A LOT OF MUD DIGGERS YOU'VE GOT, ANYWAY!

WILSON, DID YOU HEAR THAT? MUD DIGGERS, THE GENERAL CALLS US!

THE GENERAL THEN WHEELED AND RODE AWAY. LIEUTENANT HASBROUK, WHO HAD LISTENED WITH AN AIR OF IMPOTENT RAGE, SPOKE SUDDENLY IN FIRM TONES...

I DON'T CARE WHAT A MAN IS--WHETHER A GENERAL OR WHAT--IF HE SAYS THE BOYS DIDN'T PUT UP A GOOD FIGHT, HE'S A DARN FOOL!

LIEUTENANT, THIS IS MY AFFAIR AND I'LL TROUBLE YOU TO KEEP OUT OF IT.

MUD DIGGERS, HUH! WHAT DOES HE THINK WE WERE DOIN' OUT THERE--PLAYIN' MARBLES?

JUST THEN, SOME MEN CAME RUNNING UP...

HEY, FLEMING! WILSON! WAIT TILL YOU HEAR THE NEWS!

WHAT IS IT?

COLONEL KENT ASKED THE LIEUTENANT WHO WAS CARRYIN' THE FLAG AND HE SAID, "THAT'S FLEMING, A REG'LAR JIMHICKY. HE AN' WILSON LED THE HULL CHARGE."

GO ON THOMPSON, YOU'RE LYIN'.

IT'S THE TRUTH! AN' THE COLONEL SAYS, "THOSE LADS DESERVE TO BE MAJOR-GENERALS."

ATTA BOY, HENRY! GUESS YOU SHOWED 'EM!

THAT'S SOMETHIN' TO WRITE HOME ABOUT, WILSON!

HIS SELF-CONFIDENCE RESTORED, HENRY STOOD PROUDLY WATCHING THE ADJOINING BRIGADE OPEN FIRE AS THE BATTLE RESUMED...

SUDDENLY, THE CONFEDERATE SOLDIERS CAME CHARGING OUT OF THE WOODS...

OFF TO ONE SIDE, HENRY AND WILSON SAW A FORMIDABLE LINE OF THE ENEMY COME WITHIN DANGEROUS RANGE. THE REBELS WERE RUNNING TOWARD A FENCE...

THEY'RE HEADIN' FOR THE FENCE! THEY'LL BE ABLE TO CUT US TO BITS FROM THERE!

DESPITE HEAVY FIRE FROM THE UNION TROOP, THE REBELS GAINED THE FENCE...

DOWN, BOYS, AND GIVE THOSE YANKEES ALL THE LEAD THEIR BELLIES WILL HOLD!

FROM THEIR VANTAGE POINT, THE GRAY-UNIFORMED REBELS BEGAN TO SLICE UP THE MEN IN BLUE.

THEY'LL WIPE US OUT IF WE STAY HERE. LOOKS LIKE THIS IS REALLY THE END. BUT I WON'T RUN AGAIN NO MATTER WHAT HAPPENS.

THE COLONEL CAME RIDING UP ALONG THE BACK OF THE LINE...

LIEUTENANT HASBROUCK, WE MUST CHARGE THEM! IF WE DON'T TAKE THAT WALL, WE'RE ALL GONERS!

HERE WAS AN OMINOUS CLANGING OVERTURE TO THE CHARGE WHEN THE SHAFTS OF THE BAYONETS RATTLED UPON THE RIFLE BARRELS. THEN, AT THE WORDS OF COMMAND, THE SOLDIERS SPRANG FORWARD IN EAGER LEAPS...

TO THE WALL, MEN! CHA-A-A-RGE!

GONE FOREVER WAS HENRY'S COWARDICE. GRAZED BY ENEMY FIRE AGAIN AND AGAIN, HE PUSHED FORWARD FEARLESSLY WITH THE OTHERS...

WILSON! THEIR FLAG! GET IT!

ATTA BOY, WILSON! WE'VE GOT IT! LET'S HEAR THE GENERAL CALL US MUD DIGGERS, NOW!

THE BATTLE, THOUGH FURIOUS, WAS SHORT-LIVED. MOST OF THE CONFEDERATE TROOPS WERE EITHER KILLED OR CAPTURED. VERY FEW MANAGED TO ESCAPE. HENRY EXPERIENCED A NEW THRILL OF ACCOMPLISHMENT AS HE WATCHED THOSE FEW RUN OFF...

GOOD WORK, LIEUTENANT! WE'VE BEATEN THEM BACK! THE FIELD IS OURS!

A FEW MINUTES LATER, THE BUGLE SOUNDED CALLING THE MEN TO LINE UP...

OH, NO!

THUNDER! HOW MUCH DO THEY THINK A MAN CAN STAND?

BUT...

IT'S GOOD NEWS THIS TIME, MEN! WE'RE BEING RELIEVED. WE'RE MOVING BACK ACROSS THE RIVER.

IT'S OVER--IT'S ALL OVER AT LAST.

A S THEY MARCHED SLOWLY BACK OVER THE FIELD ACROSS WHICH THEY HAD RUN IN SUCH A MAD SCAMPER, HENRY AGAIN THOUGHT BACK TO HIS FIRST WILD FLIGHT... BUT THE THOUGHT WAS SOON BURIED BENEATH THE KNOWLEDGE THAT HE HAD FINALLY PROVEN HIMSELF TO BE A MAN. HE HAD BEEN OUT THERE, FACE-TO-FACE WITH DEATH AND HAD FOUND THAT IT WAS, AFTER ALL, NOTHING BUT DEATH. HIS HEAD HIGH, HE WORE HIS RED BADGE OF COURAGE WITH GREAT PRIDE.

The End

AN OUTLINE HISTORY OF THE
CIVIL WAR

THE EVENTS LEADING UP TO THE CIVIL WAR HAD THEIR ORIGIN WITH THE COLONIZATION OF AMERICA...

WE NEED THESE SLAVES TO PICK OUR COTTON.

AYE, AND MEANWHILE THE MOTHER COUNTRY BUILDS A FINE SLAVE TRAFFIC.

BUT THE NORTHERN COLONIES FOUND LITTLE USE FOR THEIR SLAVES...

WE'LL GET A GOOD PRICE FOR THEM IN CHARLESTON. THEY AREN'T MUCH GOOD IN THE COLD WEATHER WE HAVE UP HERE.

BY THE 1770'S SLAVERY HAD BECOME A NECESSARY PART OF THE SOUTH'S ECONOMIC LIFE...

WHILE THE INDUSTRIALIZED NORTH BEGAN TO FROWN ON SLAVERY...

I SAY NO MAN SHOULD BE KEPT IN BONDAGE. A MAN SHOULD BE PAID FOR HIS WORK.

*A*FTER THE REVOLUTIONARY WAR, THE FIGHT BETWEEN THE NORTH AND SOUTH BEGAN FOR THE CONTROL OF CONGRESS.

THERE ARE NOW ELEVEN FREE AND ELEVEN SLAVE STATES. IF YOU LET MAINE COME IN AS A FREE STATE, THEN MISSOURI MUST COME IN AS A SLAVE STATE.

*A*S NEW STATES WERE ADDED TO THE UNION, BOTH SIDES SOUGHT TO BRING THEM TO THEIR WAY OF LIFE. ALTHOUGH THERE WERE COMPROMISES IN 1850 AND 1854, A DEEP HATRED BETWEEN THE NORTH AND SOUTH HAD DEVELOPED... JOHN BROWN, MILITANT LEADER OF THE ABOLITIONISTS, STAGED RAID AFTER RAID ON SLAVE HOLDERS IN KANSAS.

BURN THEM OUT! WE'LL HAVE NO SOUTHERN SYMPATHIZERS IN KANSAS. OUR STATE WILL COME TO THE UNION, FREE!

*T*HE BOOK "UNCLE TOM'S CABIN" FANNED THE NORTH'S HATRED OF SLAVERY...

IT'S AWFUL THE WAY THEY TREAT THOSE NEGROES DOWN THERE. YOU MEN MUST STOP THEM!

*T*HE SUPREME COURT "DRED SCOTT" CASE DECISION ALLOWING SLAVERY IN THE TERRITORIES HEIGHTENED THAT HATRED...

OUR REPUBLICAN CANDIDATE, ABRAHAM LINCOLN, IS PLEDGED TO ABOLISH SLAVERY. WE MUST ELECT HIM AND BLOT OUT THIS SHAME ON OUR FREE COUNTRY.

WITH THE CONFEDERATE CAPITOL, RICHMOND, AS ITS FIRST OBJECTIVE, THE UNION ARMY, UNDER GENERAL McDOWELL INVADED VIRGINIA AND WAS MET BY THE SOUTHERN FORCES AT BULL RUN ON JULY 21, 1861...

THE NORTH WAS ROUTED AND RETREATED TO WASHINGTON IN PANIC...

MAKE THEM COUNT, BOYS! JOHNNY REB* IS A CRACK SHOT.

*T*HERE WAS GLOOM IN WASHINGTON. LINCOLN REPLACED GENERAL McDOWELL WITH GENERAL GEORGE B. McCLELLAN...

WE LOST AT BULL RUN BECAUSE WE WERE POORLY TRAINED. I WANT MY MEN PRE-PARED FOR BATTLE, EVEN IF IT TAKES UNTIL NEXT SPRING.

*ALL CONFEDERATE SOLDIERS WERE CALLED THIS NAME BY THE UNION FORCES.

MEANWHILE, THE CONFEDERATE IRON-CLAD SHIP "MERRIMAC" HAD BEEN SINKING FEDERAL SHIPS IN CHESAPEAKE BAY...

THE UNION BUILT A METAL SHIP, THE "MONITOR", AND SENT IT AFTER THE "MERRIMAC". THE TWO METAL MONSTERS MET OFF HAMPTON ROADS, VIRGINIA, MARCH 9, 1862. THE BATTLE WAS A DRAW, BUT IT FORECAST THE EVENTUAL END OF THE WOODEN BATTLESHIP...

AND SOON HAD AN EFFECTIVE BLOCKADE AGAINST ALL THE SOUTHERN PORTS ALONG THE ATLANTIC...

THE NORTH HAD THE ABILITY AND FACILITIES TO BUILD SHIPS...

SPEED IT UP, MEN. THERE'S A BONUS IF SHE'S FINISHED IN THIRTY DAYS.

THE RATIONS KEEP GETTING SMALLER AND SMALLER.

IF THOSE YANKEE SHIPS WOULD LEAVE, OUR YOUNG ONES COULD EAT PROPERLY.

IN THE SPRING OF 1862, McCLELLAN INVADED VIRGINIA. BUT AFTER REPEATED BLUNDERS HE WAS REPLACED BY GENERAL JOHN POPE WHO MET THE REBELS AT THE SECOND BATTLE OF BULL RUN AUGUST 30, 1862...

THE TWO OPPOSING ARMIES MET AT ANTIETAM CREEK, WHERE LEE WAS CHECKED AND FORCED TO RETREAT. McCLELLAN AGAIN TOOK OVER COMMAND OF THE UNION TROOPS.

HAVING CHECKED THE YANKEES, GENERAL LEE DECIDED TO INVADE THE BORDER STATE OF MARYLAND...

MARYLAND IS SOUTHERN AT HEART. WE'LL FIND MANY ALLIES THERE TO HELP US TAKE THE STATE.

THEY DON'T SEEM TO ANSWER OUR FIRE ANY MORE.

I'LL REPORT TO McCLELLAN.

SIR, DON'T YOU THINK WE SHOULD GO AFTER LEE'S ARMY?

NO, IT'S TOO RISKY.

TWICE YOU HAVE FAILED US, GENERAL McCLELLAN. YOU SHOULD HAVE PRESSED LEE'S ARMY. I'M REPLACING YOU WITH GENERAL BURNSIDE.

To give some measure of cheer to the despairing North, President Lincoln, on January 1, 1863, issued his famous "Emancipation Proclamation", declaring free all slaves in the states then "in rebellion against the United States"...

On December 13, 1862, at Fredericksburg, Virginia, General Burnside made the costliest blunder of the Civil War...

ANOTHER ONE. THEY FALL LIKE FLIES!

THE STUPIDITY OF SENDING THEM ACROSS AN OPEN FIELD AGAINST US IN THESE TRENCHES.

THE CASUALITY LISTS ARE APPALLING ; I'VE REPLACED BURNSIDE WITH "FIGHTING JOE" HOOKER. MAYBE HE'LL BRING US A VICTORY.

Hooker met the rebels at Chancellorsville, Virginia, on May 2, 1863...

SEND THIS MESSAGE TO THE PRESIDENT: "WE WERE DEFEATED TODAY. OUR ONLY CONSOLATION IS THAT THE REBELS MISTAKENLY KILLED THEIR GENERAL, 'STONEWALL' JACKSON".

ALTHOUGH THE NORTH HAD BEEN TAKING TERRIBLE DEFEATS IN THE VIRGINIA CAMPAIGN, GENERAL ULYSSES S. GRANT HAD BEEN MAKING SLOW PROGRESS IN THE WEST...

HERE'S A MESSAGE FROM GRANT. HE HAS JUST TAKEN SHILOH AND SHALL ATTEMPT A SIEGE OF VICKSBURG. IT IS ONE OF OUR THREE MAJOR OBJECTIVES, THE OTHERS BEING RICHMOND AND CHATTANOOGA.

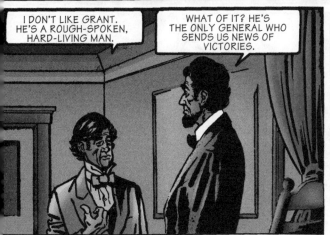

I DON'T LIKE GRANT. HE'S A ROUGH-SPOKEN, HARD-LIVING MAN.

WHAT OF IT? HE'S THE ONLY GENERAL WHO SENDS US NEWS OF VICTORIES.

AS GRANT STARTED HIS SEIGE OF VICKSBURG, LEE PREPARED TO INVADE THE NORTH. HE WAS MET AT GETTYSBURG, PENNSYLVANIA, BY GENERAL GEORGE MEADE, WHO HAD REPLACED GENERAL HOOKER.

LEE CAME ACROSS THE BLUE RIDGE MOUNTAINS IN MARYLAND...

AND UP THE SHENANDOAH VALLEY FOR A DATE WITH DESTINY...

THE BATTLE OPENED JULY 1, 1863, WITH THE NORTH OCCUPYING CEMETERY RIDGE AND THE SOUTH OCCUPYING SEMINARY RIDGE...

ON JULY 2nd, THE REBELS ATTACKED AND WERE DRIVING OUT THE YANKEES WHEN NIGHTFALL STOPPED THE HOSTILITIES.

ON THE MORNING OF JULY 3rd, LEE GAMBLED TO CRACK THE CENTER OF THE UNION LINE BY SENDING GENERAL PICKETT CHARGING IN...

THE CHARGE FAILED AND LEE WAS FORCED TO RETREAT BACK SOUTH. HAD MEADE PURSUED HIM, THE WAR WOULD HAVE BEEN QUICKLY OVER. BUT AGAIN THE UNION FORCES FAILED TO TAKE FULL ADVANTAGE OF THEIR OPPORTUNITY.

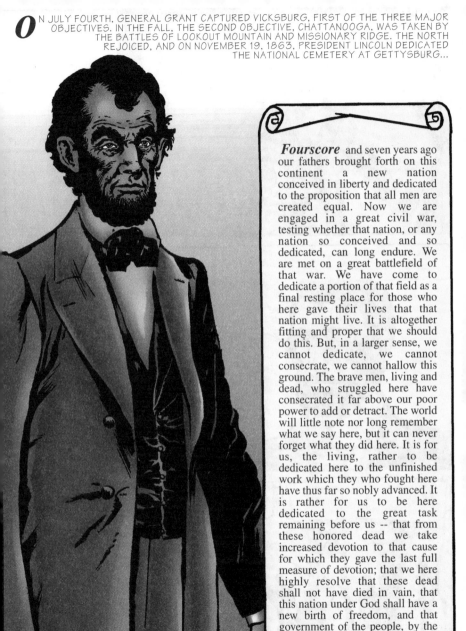

On July fourth, General Grant captured Vicksburg, first of the three major objectives. In the fall, the second objective, Chattanooga, was taken by the battles of Lookout Mountain and Missionary Ridge. The North rejoiced, and on November 19, 1863, President Lincoln dedicated the National Cemetery at Gettysburg...

Fourscore and seven years ago our fathers brought forth on this continent a new nation conceived in liberty and dedicated to the proposition that all men are created equal. Now we are engaged in a great civil war, testing whether that nation, or any nation so conceived and so dedicated, can long endure. We are met on a great battlefield of that war. We have come to dedicate a portion of that field as a final resting place for those who here gave their lives that that nation might live. It is altogether fitting and proper that we should do this. But, in a larger sense, we cannot dedicate, we cannot consecrate, we cannot hallow this ground. The brave men, living and dead, who struggled here have consecrated it far above our poor power to add or detract. The world will little note nor long remember what we say here, but it can never forget what they did here. It is for us, the living, rather to be dedicated here to the unfinished work which they who fought here have thus far so nobly advanced. It is rather for us to be here dedicated to the great task remaining before us -- that from these honored dead we take increased devotion to that cause for which they gave the last full measure of devotion; that we here highly resolve that these dead shall not have died in vain, that this nation under God shall have a new birth of freedom, and that government of the people, by the people, for the people, shall not perish from the earth.

GENERAL GRANT WAS NOW PLACED IN FULL COMMAND OF THE UNION ARMIES...

THE SOUTH IS IN A BAD WAY. HER MONEY IS ALMOST WORTHLESS, OUR BLOCKADE IS STOPPING SUPPLIES FROM REACHING HER TROOPS. SHE SUFFERS FROM SICKNESS, DISEASE AND DESERTION. CAN YOU END THE WAR QUICKLY, GENERAL?

I'LL TRY! I'LL MAKE A FRONTAL ATTACK AGAINST RICHMOND. I'LL HAVE SHERIDAN DRIVE THROUGH THE SHENANDOAH, AND SHERMAN WILL MARCH FROM CHATTANOOGA TO THE SEA.

BY THIS THREE-PRONGED DRIVE, THE SOUTH SHOULD BE SPLIT, AND RICHMOND SHOULD FALL.

BUT LEE CHECKED GRANT AT SPOTTSYLVANIA AND THE WILDERNESS...

SIR, WE'RE TRAPPED. WHAT SHALL WE DO?

MOVE FORWARD. THERE'S AN EXIT AS WELL AS AN ENTRANCE TO THIS WILDERNESS.

AFTER ITS CAPTURE, SHERMAN'S MEN PUT ATLANTA TO THE TORCH...

SHERMAN CONTINUED HIS SPIRIT-BREAKING PILLAGE OF THE SOUTH THROUGH THE CAROLINAS... ON TO SAVANNAH, GEORGIA.

DON'T SHE MAKE A PRETTY SIGHT, BURNING IN THE TWILIGHT?

THEY WON'T FORGET SHERMAN'S MARCH DOWN HERE.

THEN RICHMOND, THE FINAL OBJECTIVE, WHICH THE UNION ARMY HAD BEEN TRYING TO CAPTURE FOR FOUR YEARS FELL EASILY TO GRANT'S MEN...

*T*HE SOUTH'S SPIRIT WAS BROKEN AND LEE SURRENDERED AT APPOMATTOX COURT HOUSE, VIRGINIA, APRIL 9, 1865...

AND NOW, SIR, I SURRENDER MY SWORD.

YOU'VE BEEN A GALLANT AND NOBLE FOE, SIR, KEEP YOUR SWORD.

*W*EARY, BEATEN REBEL SOLDIERS RETURNED TO A RUINED LAND...

YOUR PAW AND BROTHER DIED IN THE WAR, AND YOUR MAW DIED HERE. JIST PINED AWAY FOR YOU.

THE LAND'S STILL LEFT. WE'LL HAVE TO BUILD ANEW.

*W*HILE THE NORTH TURNED TO THEIR LEADER, PRESIDENT ABRAHAM LINCOLN, FOR GUIDANCE...

E MUST TREAT OUR LATE OPPONENTS E MISGUIDED BROTHERS RATHER AN LIKE ONQUERED NEMIES.

ON APRIL 14, 1865 THE MAN WHO HAD PRESERVED THE UNION, AND WHO WAS THE BEST FRIEND OF THE DEFEATED SOUTH, WAS ASSASSINATED AT FORD'S THEATRE, WASHINGTON, D.C., BY A CRAZED FANATIC, JOHN WILKES BOOTH...

ABRAHAM LINCOLN'S TASK WAS TO PRESERVE THE UNION, TO PROVE THAT OURS IS A NATION, INDIVISIBLE, WITH LIBERTY AND JUSTICE FOR ALL. ALTHOUGH SOME SCARS OF THE BLOODY WAR BETWEEN THE STATES STILL REMAIN, THE DAY WILL COME WHEN THE CIVIL WAR WILL BE JUST A TRAGIC PAGE IN OUR LONG AND GLORIOUS HISTORY.

THE RED BADGE OF COURAGE
STEPHEN CRANE

The Author

"I hear the damned book *The Red Badge of Courage* is doing very well in England...I used myself up in the accursed *Red Badge*." Stephen Crane wrote these words on the last day of 1895, his frustration beginning to show at how the fame of his Civil War story was superseding all his past and present efforts at writing. Crane did in fact leave us with other work, but it is for *The Red Badge of Courage* that he has had the most recognition, from his own lifetime to the present day.

Stephen Crane was born the youngest of 14 children in 1871 in Newark, Pennsylvania, to a Methodist minister and his wife. When he was a boy, Stephen's family moved to Port Jervis, New York, near New York City. Reverend Crane died in 1880, leaving the mother to complete the task of raising her large brood. She moved the family back to New Jersey, to the seaside town of Asbury Park. Young Stephen spent his high-school years first at Pennington Seminary, which he left when a teacher accused him of lying ("the professor called me a liar so) there was not room at

Pennington for us both"), and then at the Claverack College and Hudson River Institute, a coeducational prepatory school which had a military training battalion for boys. Years later, one of Stephen's sisters-in-law remembered that "his fondness for everything military induced his mother to send him" there. From there, Crane went on to Lafayette College and then Syracuse University. However, he was not cut out for serious academic pursuit, at least not in the conventional sense; he preferred spending time with his fraternity brothers and fellow athletes (he played shortstop and catcher for both schools' teams). More importantly, Crane spent more and more time devoting himself to the career he was determined to embark upon and succeed in: writing. Previously, young Stephen had written short pieces for the small-town New Jersey newspaper edited by his older brother; now, he turned his sights and talents toward New York City. He looked beyond the university campus for his education, and embraced all manner of experiences in his attempt to come to know the world. By the time Crane left Syracuse for good, he'd already seen his byline in the prestigious New York dailies *The Herald* and *The Tribune*.

After he published his first book *Maggie: A Girl of the Streets* in 1893, Crane started on his novel of the Civil War. It was first published as serial installments in a magazine; shortly thereafter, Crane was hired as a roving correspondent by a New York City newspaper. He set off on a journey through the American West which eventually took him to Mexico. (Along the way, Crane met the young Willa Cather, who would go on to achieve her own fame as a novelist — this was the first of many acquaintances he'd make of fellow writers who were also working with the new ideas and forms he was using.) The young journalist also used the time away to revise his manuscript of *The Red Badge* in order to prepare for its publication in book form. The novel met with critical success in both the U.S. and England when it was published in 1895.

Crane's next journey was truly full of adventure. He'd been determined to actually experience war, as opposed to imagining it, as he'd done in the writing of *The Red Badge*. He set off for Florida in the hopes of securing passage to Cuba, where that island's struggle for independence from Spain would soon lead to open warfare between the U.S. and Spain.

While Crane was in Florida, he met the woman who would become his common-law wife, Cora Taylor. A month after their meeting, Crane was off to Cuba on the steamer *Commodore* — which promptly sank once she reached the high seas. Crane and three others (the captain, oiler, and cook) spent what must have seemed an eternity (actually little more than 30 hours) in the lifeboat. They did in fact make it back to the Florida coast, though the oiler was killed when he was thrown from, then struck by, the boat in the rough surf. Ironically, the man killed had been the best sailor and swimmer of the four men in the boat. To Stephen, the oiler's death pointed up the irrationality of the universe. Almost immediately after this experience, Crane set it down in a short story. Called (appropriately enough) *The Open Boat* (1897), it is one of the most powerful in American literature.

In April 1897 Stephen and Cora Crane (now traveling as a couple) went to cover a war in Greece. From there, Stephen gleefully wrote home to one of his brothers that "I expect to get a position on the staff of the Crown Prince. Won't that be great? I am so happy over it I can hardly breathe. I shall try — try like blazes to get a decoration out of the thing... What Crane witnessed in Greece later led him to tell his friend, the

reat novelist Joseph Conrad, that
he Red Badge's depiction of war
/as indeed "all right." By June of
897, the Cranes were settled in
ngland, where they were part of a
terary circle which included,
'onrad, H.G. Wells, (*The Time
1achine, The War of the Worlds*), and
ven Henry James (*The Portrait of a
ady*). The next year, Crane returned
) the United States to try to enlist in
he Navy in anticipation of the war
/ith Spain. However, due to his fail-
1g health, he was rejected; not to be
ut off from the scent of adventure,
rane got himself hired as a war cor-
:spondent for Joseph Pulitzer.
[owever, that was to be his last
rush with the dangerous thrill of
attle; afterwards, Crane lived in
ngland with Cora for most of the
me left to him. His health was dete-
orating rapidly; a vicious bout with
aberculosis finally led Cora to try to
rrange a stay for him at a spa in
ermany's Black Forest. But there
as nothing to be done: Stephen
rane died on June 5th, 1900. He
as 28.

The characters in *The Red
Badge of Courage* are notable
for their namelessness as much
as for anything else. The young
hero of the book, Henry
Fleming, is known primarily as
"the youth." Crane deliberately
indulges in this anonymity in
order to broaden the story's
1pact beyond that of a specific

young man; by doing so, we can
imagine Henry to be a stand-in for
any number of countless young men
sent off to fight a war of which they
know little. What we do know about
Henry is that he serves with the
304th New York Regiment — a fictional regiment, but probably similar
in make-up to any regiment from the
state where Crane spent much of his
life. Crane could have heard war sto-
ries from local veterans living in the
towns where his family lived, and
from that, it would not have been difficult for him to have imagined the
central three, and later peripheral,
soldiers of Henry's squad. In addition, based on his extensive reading
of war accounts, Crane's mind would
have been full of ideas from which
he could draw material for his novel.

Henry Fleming: According to
the scant information given on
Henry's home life, we hear that he is
a farmboy, but that he lives near a
town. He has attended school (called
a "seminary") in this town. He even
has fond memories of a young girl
from the school. In the first pages of
the novel we read "He had, of course,
dreamed of battles all his life—" We
can guess that Henry's nostalgia for
the girl seems to be based solely on
the hope that when he returns home,
she will be impressed by his bravery
in having gone off to war.
Apparently, Henry's father has died
some time before, and Henry's mother runs the family farm. There is not

much that we can guess about the boy's relationship with his mother, beyond supposing that he has been a dutiful son to her — so far. His first plea to her for permission to enlist is rebuffed; soon after, he goes to join up without first telling her. When he leaves home, she offers a curt blessing, showing little emotion. That's why we're taken by surprise, and moved all the more for its unexpectedness, in the description of Henry's last glimpse of his mother: "...he had seen his mother kneeling among the potato parings. Her brown face, upraised, was stained with tears, and her spare form was quivering." There is no indication of any brothers or sisters, which might explain why Henry had not joined the army earlier. In fact, we begin to see glimmers of Henry's self-absorbtion as we consider the question: who will help Henry's mother now that he is gone?

What more can we guess about Henry's personality from the story? We know he does not participate in the general round of gossiping and joking the other soldiers are indulging in as the story opens. Instead, Henry rather seems to pride himself on his ability to remove himself from the crowd, in order to ponder the meaning of his existence. Without he himself saying the words, we are led to understand that he thinks his sensibilities are of a refined nature compared to his companions. Throughout the course of the novel, we listen to Henry reason things out in his head, things that are rarely treated to spoken discussion When the moments arise in which Henry has to express himself out loud, words frequently fail him.

Wilson "The loud soldier," is in many ways Henry's alter-ego. It's safe to say that being in the same regiment, the two are from the same area. This is confirmed when Wilson gives Henry a packet of letters to deliver to his loved ones in case he i killed in battle. (Henry's plan to use these letters if Wilson questions him too closely about his 'red badge' is another indication of Henry's lack of sympathy for his comrades.) Wilson is called the "loud soldier" to distinguish him from Jim Conklin, called the "tall soldier." Both men are described at their first encounter in this way to help establish the tone of the scene, which, as we've seen, is meant to indicate a general campground peopled by nameless soldiers. Later, Wilson's character undergoes a change and he is no as argumentative as before, but Cran still refers to him as the "loud" sol-

ier. In the last battle, Wilson again erves as a foil (or opposite) for Ienry, when they are both struggling o hold aloft the regimental flags. 'irst, both Henry and Wilson lunge or their own flag when the sergeant arrying it is killed; Henry succeeds n grabbing and holding on to it. 'hen, Wilson gets the enemy flag vhen the Jnion side verruns the .ebel strong-old. Whether Vilson and Ienry are seen s opponents, each trying to outdo ie other, or whether they are seen as ue comrades-in-arms, marching longside each other with their flags 'aving together in the breeze, each f the two men serve to highlight the haracter of the other.

Jim Conklin: Jim Conklin is iemorable, sadly, for is grotesque dance of eath. This section of ie novel has drawn iuch attention, and ghtfully so. Crane aints a portrait of a ian dying of a horri-ble wound, a man making the leap over the great chasm which divides this world from the next one. All Henry, and anyone else can do, is watch in horror as Jim, like some maddened bull in the ring, goes stumbling off to die. Alone.

The Tattered Man: Witness to Jim's death along with Henry is the tattered man, a soldier who befriends Henry after the youth has run from the battle. The man knows nothing of Henry's flight, or of his shame, so all of his seemingly innocent commentary is like a double-edged sword to Henry. The soldier keeps inquiring how Henry received his wound, where on his body was he wounded, and to which company he belongs. Maddened by the man's questions, Henry runs off.

The Lieutenant. We also meet the young lieutenant of Henry's company, who is described as beating his own men in order to get them to fight and hold their line during the first run in. As this is exactly the moment Henry comes to the conclusion that the only sane thing he can do is to turn tail and run, it'd seem as if the lieutenant and Henry had little

The Civil War: A Pop Culture Event

Since the time that followed Lee's surrender at Appomattox, portraying, representing, and selling the Civil War in various forms and genres has been a hot-ticket item. Right after the war, there was the publication of real-life accounts such as General Abner Doubleday's (he of baseball fame) volume (*Chancellorsville and Gettysburg*) and Charles E. Benton's *As Seen From the Ranks* (an account of a New York regiment much like Henry's fictional 304th). Nowadays, we have full-scale Civil War battle re-enactments — with paying audiences videotaping it all for a new posterity. The Civil War has been a part of our cultural imagination, and will probably hold its place for generations to come. Just last year, the Disney Company had to forgo plans to build a theme park on the site of one of Virginia's many Civil War battlefields.

Perhaps it is fitting that one of Hollywood's earliest and biggest successes had to do with this national rite-of-passage. *Birth of a Nation* (1915) was the film version of a popular play called *The Clansman*, which told the story of the founding of the Ku Klux Klan. It may be no surprise that the Klan's members are made out to be heroes — the playwright Thomas Dixon and the filmmaker D. W. Griffith were Southerners, and the movie is unabashedly Confederate in its sympathies (Griffith's father had been a colonel in the Southern army).

The film is most important for re-introducing the Civil War into 20th century American culture, though it is difficult to admire because of its overtly racist message. In the 20 years that followed that film's release, the film industry grew in size and influence. By the time it was announced in the late 1930s that Hollywood was seeking an actress to play the lead in the film version of Margaret Mitchell's best-selling novel of Civil War Georgia, a publicity frenzy had already erupted nationwide. With its beguiling heroine Scarlett O'Hara, *Gone With the Wind* became one of Hollywood's most successful films ever, not just financially, but in terms of its place in the cultural imagination. Unfortunately, this movie is also severely dated in its portrayal of blacks; when its sequel was made a few years ago, the producers had to find a balance between maintaining the integrity of the story and using material that was not offensive by today's standards of racial tolerance.

The middle decades of the century did not see many films produced on the Civil War, though it is interesting to note that one was John Huston's version of *The Red Badge of Courage*, made in 1951. This film captures few of the subtleties in Crane's book, but it does a good job in showing the coming-of-age story. It was only in the late 1980s that the film industry started to pay serious attention to the War, perhaps because of its relation to the two major public issues of the latter half of our century, the Civil Rights movement and the Vietnam War.

Interestingly, the first major Civil War film of our era dealt with a little-examined aspect of the war's history: *Glory* (1989) is based on the exploits of the all-black 54th Massachusetts Regiment, a unit explicitly formed so blacks could serve as *soldiers*, rather than just gravediggers and mule-drivers. At first, the 54th was kept from participating in battle, but due to the insistence of their own officer, Colonel Robert Gould Shaw, and men such as Frederick Douglass, they were finally allowed to take part in the assault on Charleston's Fort Wagner. It was almost a foregone conclusion that the well-defended fort would be able to repulse such an attack, but it is a testament to the commitment of the soldiers of the 54th that some of their number did succeed in scaling the fort's walls. Half of the regiment died in the attack, including Colonel Shaw, whose body was contemptuously thrown in a common grave with those of his fellow soldiers. To the Confederates, he was not worthy of the officer's privilege of being buried in a separate grave; years later, when Shaw's family were asked if they cared to retrieve his body for re-burial, they replied he would have wanted to be buried with his men, and so his remains were left undisturbed. *Glory* is also notable for its concise and unforgiving portrayal of the hor-rors of close fighting. Just as Crane describes in his book, in *Glory* we see a mist divide the two armies, only to see it lift, revealing the Confederate line a few short yards from the Union line. The film *Gettysburg* (1993) delves into the personalities of some of the Union and Confederate military leaders fighting that day, as it focuses on the battle that was the turning point of the war. The film does an excellent job of portraying the battle as it unfolded over the period of several days in a small town in southern Pennsylvania.

Certainly the most innovative film treatment to date has been Ken Burns's *The Civil War*. This documentary used only still photographs, interviews with modern historians, and voiceovers of actors reading from contemporary accounts of people (including politicians, businessmen, slaves, women and ordinary soldiers) from both the North and South. Burns's film moved the nation's viewers when it was shown on television in the early 90s, in large part because it spoke to people of all sympathies and interests, Union and Confederate, black and white, military buff and student. By having as its main narrative focus the letters written by one Union and one Confederate soldier, Burns's work achieved an utter simplicity of tone which belied its intense look at a series of complex issues. That is where *The Red Badge of Courage* succeeds as well. Its seeming simplicity hides its range of issues.

in common. However, later on in the series of engagements, he and Henry become alike in their desire to meet, fight, and conquer the enemy.

The General:

Towards the end of the story, eavesdropping in the company of Henry and Wilson, we get to overhear the division's general say that the 304th fight "like a lot "a mule drivers," which the soldiers take as a deep insult. (But they do not in fact perform the job they were sent to do, so whose opinion is right, the general's or Henry and his friends'?) Crane once again shows his care not to introduce too many characters of authority, or at least not for too long a period of time. We are meant to experience the battle in the same way that Henry and his friends do, without any insight into the overall battle strategy.

The Negro Teamster:

Conspicuous by their absence are any characters who might suggest the greater political concerns behind the war. That's why the only mention of a black character is a brief one. The Negro teamster is described in the fourth paragraph of the novel, and no more. He is dancing for the amusement of the men of Henry's camp. Crane deliberately did not delve into the deeper moral and ethical issues

of the socio-political causes of the war; he was more interested in the personal morality of Henry Fleming. To have given a realistic portrait of the political causes of the war would have been misleading to his purpose; more specifically, to have given a farmboy like Henry the awareness of issues such as Emancipation, issues that had probably never touched his life, would have been a false and forced thing for the author to do. Stephen Crane believed that art should not preach; he felt that above all else, art's responsibility was to be sincere.

Plot

Imagine yourself hundreds of miles away from home, when previously 20 miles was considered a terrific journey to make. Imagine fighting in a war that is fought, according to the politicians, for lofty purposes and noble aims, but to you seems to be conducted without reason or logic. Imagine that you play out in your head dreams of achieving glory in that war, but that those dreams are rudely interrupted by the jokes and comments of your fellow soldiers, who sit bored and restless in the camp you've all been stranded in for a seeming eternity. Then, imagine that you suddenly get the chance to prove yourself in battle, a great battle that takes place all around you, but where you cannot guess what the surrounding landscape looks like just beyond your line of vision. You cannot tell whether it's an enemy soldier or a friendly one who will be the next person to face you. Finally, imagine that it is this uncertainty that leads you to do what you

never thought you'd do — turn and run, run for your sanity, and for your very life. This is the experience of a young Union soldier fighting in the Civil War, as rendered in swift but subtle strokes from the pen of Stephen Crane in *The Red Badge of Courage*.

We *can* imagine this scenario by reading Crane's little gem of a war novel, because we undergo the emotions and perceptions of such a person — Crane draws a portrait of the inner-workings of the young soldier's psyche (a word that can mean soul, spirit, *and* mind), so that we feel the things he feels, we see the things he sees, and we triumph when he does. Shortly before he started work on *The Red Badge*, Crane talked with a friend who also wished to be a writer. The friend expressed his frustration with trying to depict experience through words. Crane scooped up a handful of sand, and tossed it into the wind, saying,

"Treat your notions like that. Forget what you think about it and tell how you feel about it. Make the other fellow know you are just as human as he is. That's the big secret of story-telling. Away with literary fads and canons. Be yourself!" Some time soon after this, Crane was poring over *The Century Illustrated Magazine*, popular at that time, which was running a series of articles on the Civil War. In Crane's response to the accounts of the war which he read in the articles, we can see how he was beginning to think of writing his own war story: "I wonder that some of those fellows don't tell how they *felt* in those scraps. They spout enough of what they *did*, but they're as emotionless as rocks." Crane was familiar with the Russian writer Leo Tolstoy's account of a battle in the Crimean War, and had also read some of the French writer Emile Zola's war writings; now he felt ready to make his own contribution to this type of literature. Stephen Crane started work on the first draft of *Red Badge* in June 1893, not yet 22 years old.

The Red Badge of Courage is probably based on the Battle of Chancellorsville, fought in May 1863, shortly before the Battle of

Gettysburg. The Union accounts of the battle tell of soldiers getting lost in the dense ground vegetation, and of confusion among the ranks as to where they were going at any given time. This battle was probably General Lee's last great victory for the South, but it was a battle won at great cost: his second-in-command, General "Stonewall" Jackson, was mistakenly shot by one of his own pickets, and died a few days later.

This then, is an approximation of where we find young Henry Fleming awaiting news of his first battle. The novel opens with his regiment, the 304th New York, camped out along the hillsides, waiting on commanders' orders. The regiment is made up of raw recruits, all of whom are both nervous and anxious to see war up close. (The more seasoned veterans call out "fresh fish, fresh fish," and later laugh at how 304th actually fights the battle.) There is much grumbling around the campfire, with one man ("the tall soldier") claiming to know where they are all headed, and another soldier ("the loud soldier") swearing just as quickly the opposite to be true. In the midst of this, Henry sits alone and frets about whether or not he'll run when he goes into battle for the first time. He wonders why no one else seems to be bothered by this question, and comes

to the conclusion that none of them are as sensitive, or sensible, as he, and that therefore they don't think of these things, or might not have the natural intelligence to get going if the going gets tough. He at least agrees with his comrades on the inadequacy of their commanding officers; all of the recruits think the could do a better job by far of running the army and the war. In fact, i you've read the backup section, "Ar Outline History of the Civil War" section, you might come to the sam conclusion!

Finally, the troops are ordered to move out, though this turns out to b something of a false alarm. This move only serves to aggravate the men more; Henry works himself int an even higher state of despair over the state of things. When he sees th small meadow surrounded by dense forest that they will probably fight i he grows angry at the Union leader for bringing their men to what Henr considers to be a deathtrap.

Eventually, the soldiers are told to dig in positions at the line of woods. Henry's friend Wilson (the "loud" soldier) reveals his fear of being killed, and entrus some letters to Henry to be delivered to his fam ly should Wilson die. Soon, the Rebel soldiers charge — and Henry's unit stands firm. But th jubilation is short. Although they held for the first onslaught, when the Rebs return, Henry's line melts away. He sees everyone running, and all of his natural instincts to run which had been sublimated in the short sweet moment of apparent victory now come to the fore again, and Henry joins the exodus *away* from the battle. All the while, his old self-justifying reasons for running play through his head. He has just convinced himself of the moral weight of his side of the argument, when he overhears two Union officer discuss how their side had won the skirmish. Henry is suddenly ashamed of what he did; naturally, he then tries all the harder to prove that he is right. He sees a squirrel up in a tree, and throws a pine cone at it. When the squirrel runs away in fear, Henry congratulates himself for having only acted according to the laws of nature. When something threatens you, run away. Fast. Unfortunately, Henry's woes continue to haunt him, even in a place which seemed peaceful enough. It is "a place where the high, arching boughs made a chapel." Almost immediately, near the "threshold" of this country "chapel" he stumbles across the body of a dead soldier, who is looking straight at Henry. Once again, Henry turns and runs.

He then comes across his friend Jim Conklin (the "tall" soldier) who has been mortally wounded. Despite Henry's efforts to help him, Jim staggers on alone, until he has no strength left. Conklin sinks to his knees, and dies, as Henry watches in despair. Henry leaves soon after, to escape the questioning of a soldier who wants to know what part of the battle Henry was in — a conversation Henry wishes to avoid for obvious reasons. Again he flees one uncomfortable situation, only to land in an even more uncomfortable one. Remember, Henry is in strange country; he has no gun, and has no idea where his unit is — if he can even go back. In a panic, he stops to question a retreating Union soldier about the battle; the man doesn't want to stop, so when Henry doesn't move out of the way fast enough, the impatient soldier hits Henry on the head with a rifle butt. And so Henry receives his red badge of courage.

He makes his way back to his own unit, where they accept his story that he was grazed in the head by a bullet. He never reveals how he turned and ran away from the battle, nor how he really got his head wound. Soon, he has proved himself in more skirmishes, and by the end

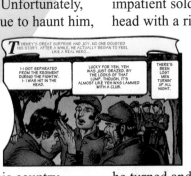

of the story, Henry is proudly carrying the regimental colors. Whether or not he honorably earned any glory through his actions is up to each person to decide as they sit and read the whole story of Henry's red badge of courage.

Interestingly, not all Civil War veterans were impressed with Crane's work. Some, who felt the portrayal of the youth and his flight dishonored the reputation of all soldiers, and in particular those who'd fought in the war, spoke out against the critical acclaim Crane received. One retired officer, reviewing the book, titled his article "The Red Badge of Hysteria." Despite the odd voice of contemporary disapproval, we can admire Crane's work for the masterpiece in miniature that it is.

Themes

Henry Fleming is at once the traditional hero who marks his passage from boy to man by a story's end, and also an *anti-hero*, whose actions disappoint conventional expectations of heroic behavior. Crane's depiction of such a protagonist (main character) indicates the author's ironic view of the customary concept of the "hero." Henry Fleming is related to each of us — we all have aspects of the hero *and* the anti-hero in us. Stephen Crane said "I evaded them (detail-oriented critics, such as veterans) in the *Red Badge* because it was essential that I should make my battle a type and name no names..." Crane imagined such types saying things like "This damned young fool was not there. I was however. And this is how it happened." However, one ex-officer, who was so taken by the novel's seemingly truthful details that he was sure its author *must* have fought in the war, claimed, "I was with Crane at Antietam." Crane was only born six years after the war ended.

The Vietnam War is now a part of our modern national consciousness, our collective history—and that is how the Civil War was perceived by late 19th century America, Crane's America. The Civil War was the first test, as a nation, of who we were as that nation. (Remember, in 1861 it'd been less than 100 years since the signing of the Declaration of Independence and the ratification of the Constitution.) In the Civil War there were tragic cases of brothers fighting brothers, mothers seeing sons fighting for a hated enemy, enslaved people fighting to be free: the growing pains of the nation were almost too much for the nation to bear. A comparative look at the effects that the Civil War had on its time and those that the Vietnam War had on our own bears some striking similarities. For one thing, there was discontent on the part of the public, as well as the ordinary soldier's, in regard to the way the war was being fought. There was good reason — the Union assault at Fredericksburg esulted in 9000 men killed, after the Union commanders sent their troops against a fortified, entrenched Confederate line a staggering *fourteen* times (see the "An Outline History of the Civil War"). One Union soldier said they were fighting "battles that produce no results," while another disillusioned Northern soldier said "until we have good generals it is useless to fight good battles. However, the soldiers were not without a sense of humor — one man referred to one of the war's early engagements, the First Battle of Bull Run (so-called by the Union, but called the First Battle of Manassas by the Confederates), as "the great skedaddle," in reference to the hurried and harried retreat of the Northern troops. Like Henry Fleming, these soldiers had less of a sense of the great picture (geographic and moral), and more of a sense of the up-close and personal picture of war. The soldiers saw just how fatal war's absurdity can be.

In military terms, the Civil War ushered in the transition between older forms of fighting and modern means of warfare. It was the first war to use repeating-fire weapons—yet battle formations still existed in which lines of men stood facing each other, sometimes mere yards apart, as they fired these new weapons. Unfortunately, ideas of battle formation changed slower than innovation for weaponry. The war introduced trench warfare, ironclad ships, and even an early version of the submarine. In "An Outline History of the Civil War," we see that the battle between the Union's *Monitor* and the South's *Merrimac* may have single-handedly ended the day of the wooden battleships. It was the first war to establish large-scale field hospitals; the Union had many more of these than its enemy did, thanks to the North's superior material wealth and to the extraordinary foresight and efforts of people such as nurse/organizers Clara Barton and Dorothea Dix. Even one of America's greatest poets, Walt Whitman, served as a nurse in a Washington D.C. hospital. Sadly, despite these advances in medical treatment, for every man killed in battle in the Civil War, two died from disease. (In fact, more men died in the Civil War than did in Vietnam.) It was the first war to be documented so thoroughly by photography, which had just recently come into its own as an artistic medium. Mathew Brady, a successful New York City portrait photographer, spent his own money outfitting traveling darkrooms, which were wagons supplied with the equipment and chemicals necessary to produce photographs of the carnage left in the aftermath of battles. (Remember, this was in the day when the photographic image was produced on glass plates, heavier and far more expensive to work with than our modern negative strip and prints.) Brady bankrupted himself in doing this historically important job; after the war, the public lost interest in his work. At one point, in order to raise cash, he sold many of his glass plates to be used as tiles for greenhouse roofs. Fortunately for us, enough of his collection survives to give us a moving and disturbingly beautiful record of the great conflict.

Although Stephen Crane wrote a truly timeless novel, it is important to understand why he chose to set his story during the Civil War. *The Red Badge of Courage* addresses an important time in our history, but just as importantly, it addresses profound questions of self-knowledge and self-consciousness in ways that speak to us in this modern era. The late 19th century saw a rise in a new type of novel, called the psychological novel, that focused on these questions. What makes Crane's book so worthy of study is its union of achievement in the historical and literary fields. Just as the Civil War was a turning point in American history, so was the psychological

novel a turning point in the history of literature.

We've seen how Henry Fleming is not the typical hero. Previous to the late 19th century, the role of the hero depended on the idea of free will: the hero made the choice to act as he did (historically, heroic literature focused on men, though myths and folktales occasionally showcase the exploits of a woman), based on his ability to distinguish right from wrong. However, in order to do this the hero needed complete self-knowledge, that is, in order to know right from wrong in the world at large, the hero needed to recognize right from wrong within himself. But if we read of Henry that "He was forced to admit that as far as war was concerned he knew nothing of himself," how can we think Henry Fleming capable of bearing the responsibility of being a hero? The narrator notes that Henry answers his own question with the charge to "accumulate information of himself." By the time Stephen Crane was writing, people were coming to believe an absolute self-knowledge impossible to achieve. In the mid-19th

HERE THEY COME!

I HOPE I DON'T RUN -- I HOPE I DON'T RUN.

entury, the ideas of Charles Darwin, t first applied only to nature, were being applied to society and its practices. We are all probably familiar with the phrase "survival of the fittest," but we must recall a time when that phrase, and the idea behind t, was new (not to mention shocking). These ideas were deeply upsetting to the traditions which for thousands of years had regulated the course of society, and which had dictated how nature was viewed in relation to society.

In addition to revolutions in the world of science, there were radical developments in the worlds of philosophy and intellectual inquiry. There was greater awareness of the irrationality in the workings of the human mind, and of the idea that the unconscious mind might play a part in dictating people's motives and actions. The American philosopher William James published his groundbreaking study *The Principles of Psychology* in 1890, while over in Europe, Sigmund Freud would publish his important work *The Interpretation of Dreams* in 1899. The public became obsessed with notions of madness and irrationality, both on a human scale and on a grander scale. This was the age when the medical establishment diagnosed hysteria as a leading illness of women (no doubt they were vindicated by the great number of women who fainted from their too-tight corsets) and

when it founded mental institutions in great numbers. Science identified the woes of society, and also identified the cures for those woes. It never occurred to anyone to question "progress" by wondering whether or not science may have even "invented" some of these woes.

Coincidentally (and probably ironically), this was also the heyday of the Industrial Era. All of a sudden, the "natural order of things," whether it was in nature, politics, culture or religion, seemed suspect at best, chaotic at worst. Just as man was showing his might (and exercising his will) over nature through the triumph of mechanization, nature itself was seen as even more capricious and liable to chance than ever before. (Perhaps the most famous example came at the twilight of this era: the great ship *Titanic*, said to be unsinkable even by God, sank in 1912 on her maiden voyage across the Atlantic.) This epic struggle of man over nature became man versus machine, man combatting the very monster he'd created (as Dr. Frankenstein battled his monster in Mary Shelley's novel *Frankenstein*.). This struggle was interpreted in many ways. Sometimes it seemed as if man should *become* a part of the machine, and only by assuming some of those qualities could man hope to survive.

One of the most famous images from *The Red Badge of Courage* comes when Henry is about to join the fight for the first time with the rest of his regiment. Suddenly, he realizes that it is simply not he, nor any other individual soldier, who is marching into battle: instead, he feels the presence of a huge mechanized being. It is useless to try to break away: "But he instantly saw that it would be impossible for him to escape the regiment. It inclosed him. And there were iron laws of tradition and law on four sides. He was in a moving box." With that statement, Crane also shows how the forces of tradition have been taken over by the newer force which rules nature, the machine. In a reverse representation, sometimes industrial, mechanical, or military structures were seen as having human or animal characteristics; use of this device is called anthropomorphism. Crane continually describes the entire regiment as one living body, deftly noting one time that "the army again sat down to think." Indeed, the second image we see in the whole book is that of an army which "awakened, and began to tremble with eagerness at the noise of rumors," as if it were a young boy ready for play. In the opening chapters of the book, Henry feels himself at one with the army, that he was not a man, but "a member," a "little piece of the army." At another point, we hear that "It seemed now that Nature had no ears," which upsets us, first because we're concerned to get this news, and second we realize that we've been sold the idea that Nature has ears without even having been aware of the author's verbal trick. Crane constantly shifts identities between man, machine, and nature.

The illustrated version of the novel that you read in this book was published a long time ago. The editors had to make some difficult decisions about which part of the text they wanted to include, and which they had to cut. As you can see, the illustrated version contains a lot of dialogue. In the novel, much of the text is actually in the "narrative voice," that is, it's in the voice of an impersonal narrator. It is important remember that this narrator is *not* Henry; often in the book, the text will read "Henry thought" or "Henry imagined," but that doesn't mean it's as if it were Henry himself speaking directly to us. For one thing, the narrator has a much better range of vocabulary than Henry would have. For another, the narrator can see things, such as a view of the whole brigade, that Henry cannot. (The narrator notes at one point that Jim makes "a fine use of the third person" — is Crane playfully pointing out his own talents to us?) This narrator's part plays a much smaller voice in the illustrated version of the novel.

NO WAY OUT NOW. I'M TRAPPED... IT'S LIKE BEING IN A MOVING BOX.